S0-BDL-865

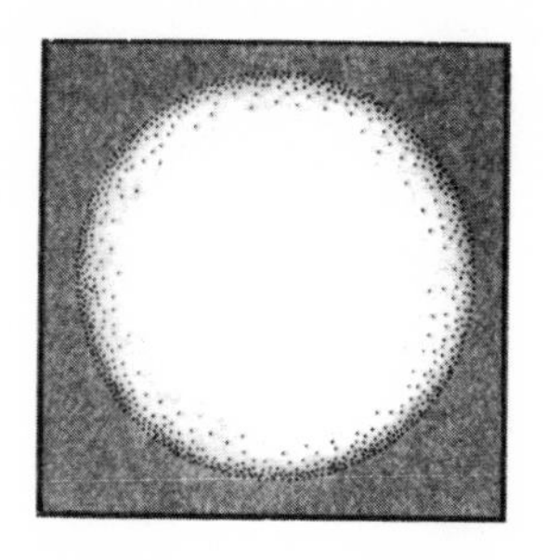

THE MOON'S THE NORTH WIND'S COOKY

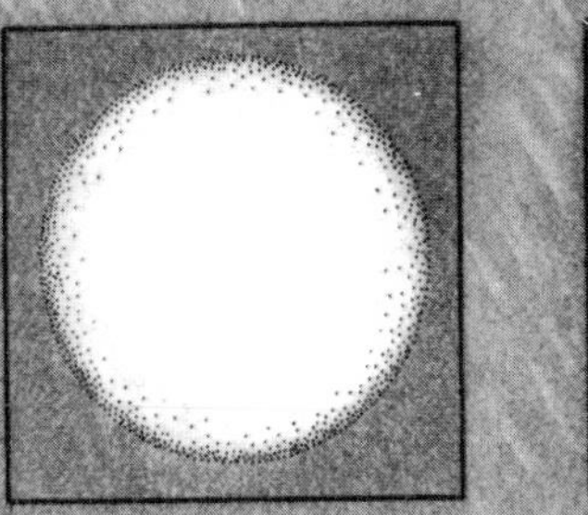
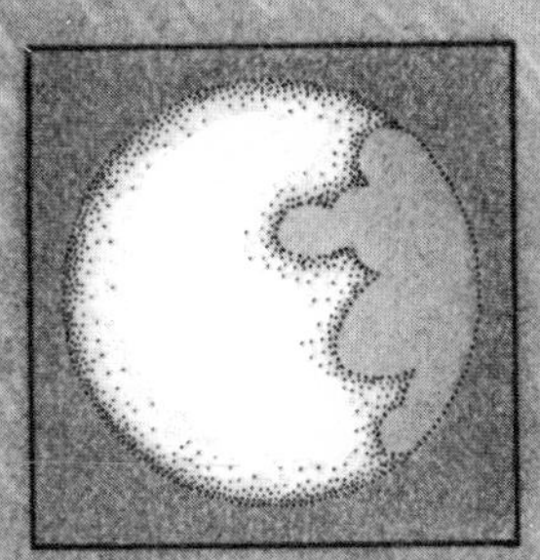

THE MOON'S THE

Night Poems

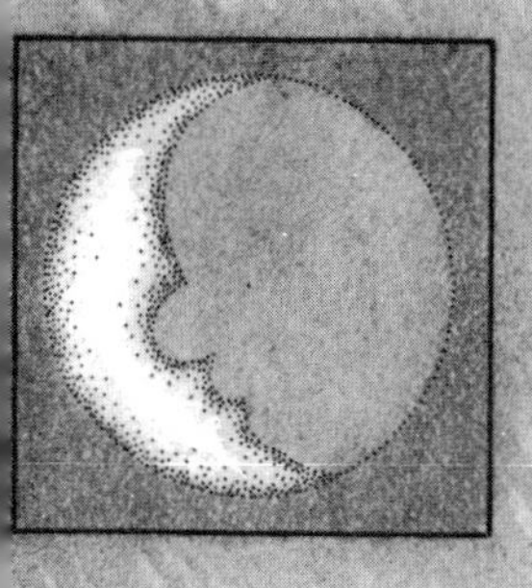
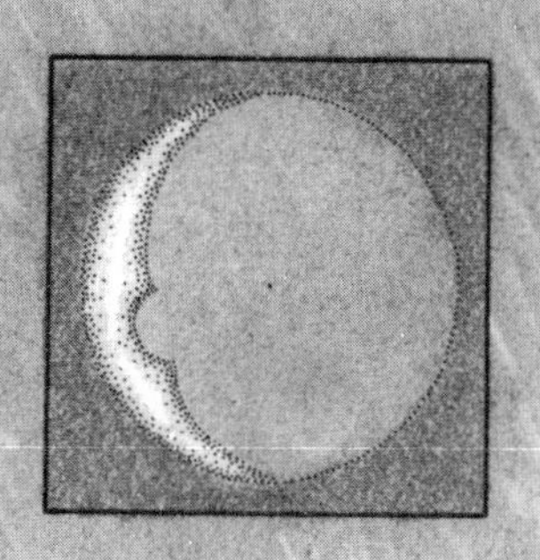
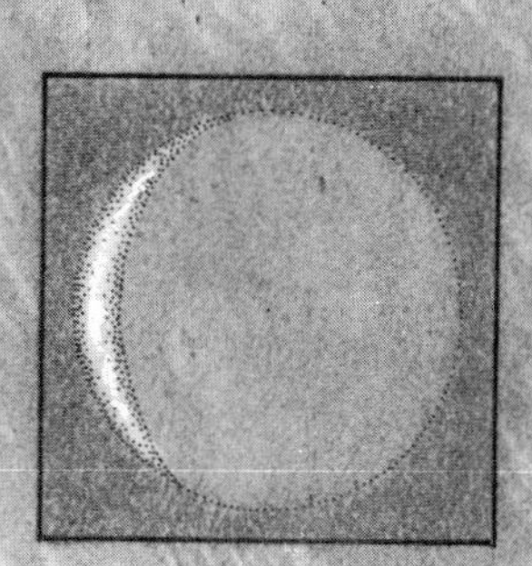

NORTH WIND'S COOKY

selected and illustrated by SUSAN RUSSO

Lothrop, Lee & Shepard Company
A Division of William Morrow & Company Inc. New York

Thanks are due to the following for permission to reprint poems in this book: Addison-Wesley Publishing Company, Inc. for "My Own Room" from *Blueberries Lavender* by Nancy Dingman Watson, Copyright © 1977 by Nancy Dingman Watson./Frank Marshall Davis for stanza three from "Four Glimpses of Night," reprinted by permission of the author./E.P. Dutton for "Night Travel" from *Rhymes About Us* by Marchette Chute, Copyright © 1974 by Marchette Chute./Nikki Giovanni for "Goodnight," reprinted by permission of the author./Harcourt Brace Jovanovich, Inc. for "Questions at Night" from *Rainbow in the Sky* edited by Louis Untermeyer, Copyright © 1935 by Harcourt Brace Jovanovich, Inc., renewed 1963 by Louis Untermeyer./Harper & Row, Publishers, Inc. for "Full of the Moon" from *In the Middle of the Trees* by Karla Kuskin, Copyright © 1958 by Karla Kuskin./Macmillan Publishing Company, Inc. for "The Moon's the North Wind's Cooky" from *Collected Poems* by Vachel Lindsay, Copyright 1914 by Macmillan Publishing Company, Inc., renewed 1942 by Elizabeth C. Lindsay./McIntosh & Otis, Inc. for "The Night" from *Whispers and Other Poems* by Myra Cohn Livingston, Copyright © 1958 by Myra Cohn Livingston./The New Yorker Magazine, Inc., for "River Night" by Frances Frost, Copyright © 1930, 1958 by The New Yorker Magazine, Inc./Louise H. Sclove for "Nocturne" from *The Light Guitar* by Arthur Guiterman, Copyright 1923 by Harper & Row, Publishers, Inc./Charles Scribner's Sons for "Night Sounds" from *At the Top of My Voice* by Felice Holman, Copyright © 1970 by Felice Holman./Viking Penguin, Inc. for "Night Landscape" from *The Skin Spinners* by Joan Aiken, Copyright © 1960, 1973, 1974, 1975, 1976 by Joan Aiken, all rights reserved.

 Inquiries should be addressed to Lothrop, Lee & Shepard Company, 105 Madison Ave., New York, N. Y. 10016. Printed in the United States of America.
First Edition 1 2 3 4 5 6 7 8 9 10

Library of Congress Cataloging in Publication Data
Main entry under title: The Moon's the North Wind's Cooky.
SUMMARY: A collection of 14 images of night by such poets as Nikki Giovanni, Louis Untermeyer, and Felice Holman.
1. Night—Juvenile poetry. 2. Children's poetry, American. 3. Children's poetry, English. [1. Night—Poetry. 2. American poetry—Collections] I. Russo, Susan.
PS595 .N54M66 811'.008 78-32178 ISBN 0-688-41879-1 ISBN 0-688-51879-6 lib. bdg.

CONTENTS

To Granny

GOODNIGHT

Goodnight Mommy
Goodnight Dad

I kiss them as I go

Goodnight Teddy
Goodnight Spot

The moonbeams call me so

I climb the stairs
Go down the hall
And walk into my room

My day of play is ending
But my night of sleep's in bloom

Nikki Giovanni

YOU'VE NO NEED TO LIGHT A NIGHT LIGHT

You've no need to light a night light
On a light night like tonight,
For a night light's light's a slight light,
And tonight's a night that's light.
When a night's light, like tonight's light,
It is really not quite right
To light night lights with their slight lights
On a light night like tonight.

Author Unknown

THE NIGHT

The night
creeps in
around my head
and snuggles down
upon the bed,
and makes lace pictures
on the wall
but doesn't say a word at all.

Myra Cohn Livingston

MY OWN ROOM

Up in my bedroom
On a winter's night
The fir tree ticks the window
When I put out the light

The sky is black and cold
The stars flash bright
The moon and clouds roll by
On the windy winter's night

I shiver as I watch
And I wish on a star
The first or the brightest
Or the one that blinks afar

And after I have wished
I jump into bed
And the fir tree ticks the window
All night by my head

But when a storm is raging
Or I hear an owl call
I like to know my brother
Is right down the hall.

Nancy Dingman Watson

THE MOON'S THE NORTH WIND'S COOKY

(What the Little Girl Said)

The moon's the North Wind's cooky
He bites it, day by day,
Until there's but a rim of scraps
That crumble all away.

The South Wind is a baker.
He kneads clouds in his den,
And bakes a crisp new moon *that . . . greedy*
North . . . Wind . . . eats . . . again!

Vachel Lindsay

RIVER NIGHT

Frances Frost

Up and down the river
The barges go:
Whether moons are yellow,
Whether stars flow
Softly over city,
Softly over town,
Sleepily the barges
Go up and down.

Up and down the river
On summer nights
The barges drift,
And emerald lights
And crimson prick
The darkness under
Blown-out stars
And gathering thunder.

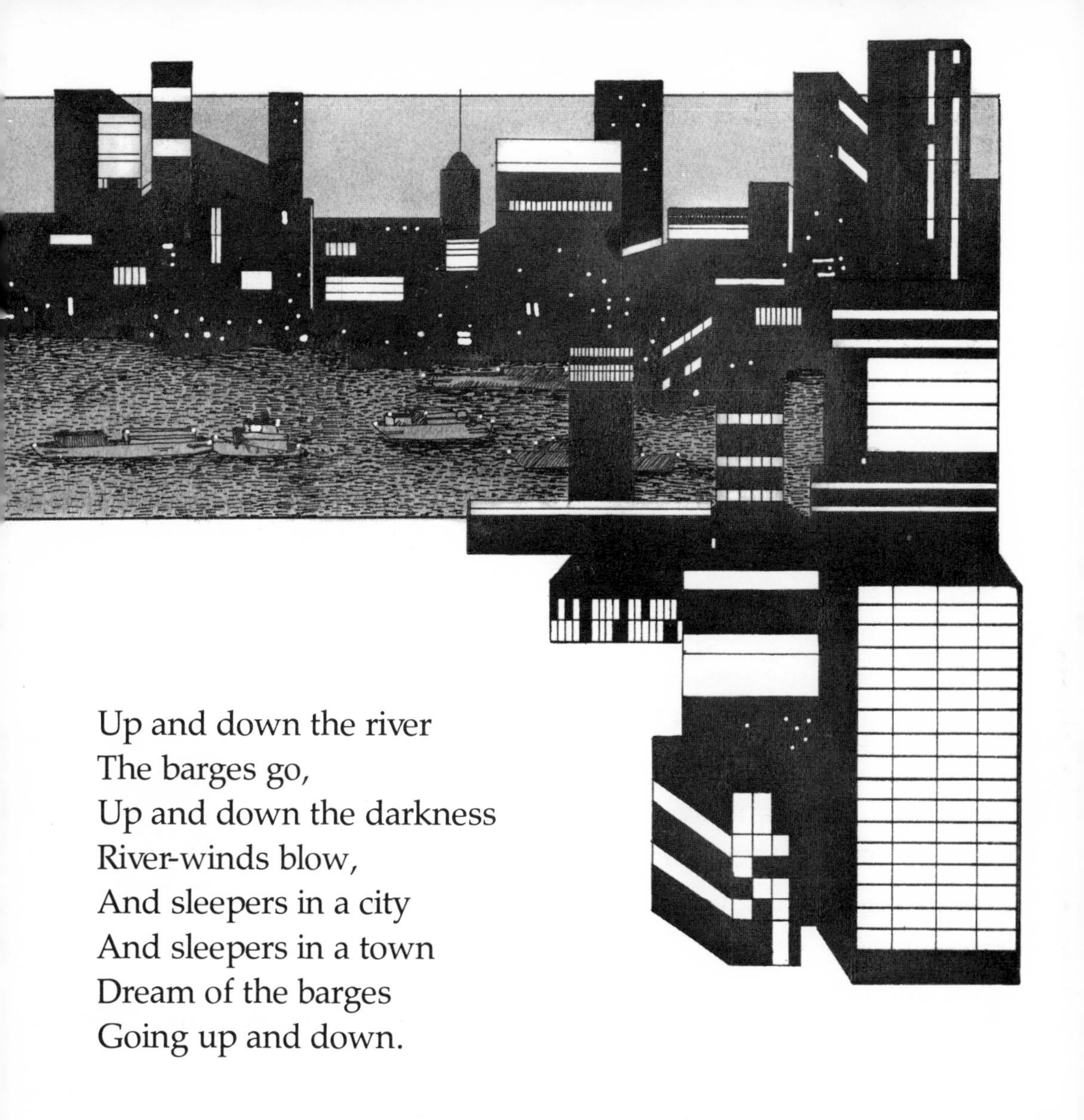

Up and down the river
The barges go,
Up and down the darkness
River-winds blow,
And sleepers in a city
And sleepers in a town
Dream of the barges
Going up and down.

NIGHT SOUNDS

In the street
    sounds of wheels humming,
    sounds of heels drumming.
Humming and drumming,
Keeping me from sleeping.
In the house
    sounds of words mumbling,
    overheard grumbling.
Mumbling and grumbling,
Keeping me unsleeping.
Far away
    sounds of waves lashing,
    quietly crashing.
Lashing and crashing,
Sweeping me to sleep.

Felice Holman

FULL OF THE MOON

It's full of the moon
The dogs dance out
Through brush and bush and bramble.
They howl and yowl
And growl and prowl.
They amble, ramble, scramble.
They rush through brush.
They push through bush.
They yip and yap and hurr.
They lark around and bark around
With prickles in their fur.
They two-step in the meadow.
They polka on the lawn.
Tonight's the night
The dogs dance out
And chase their tails till dawn.

Karla Kuskin

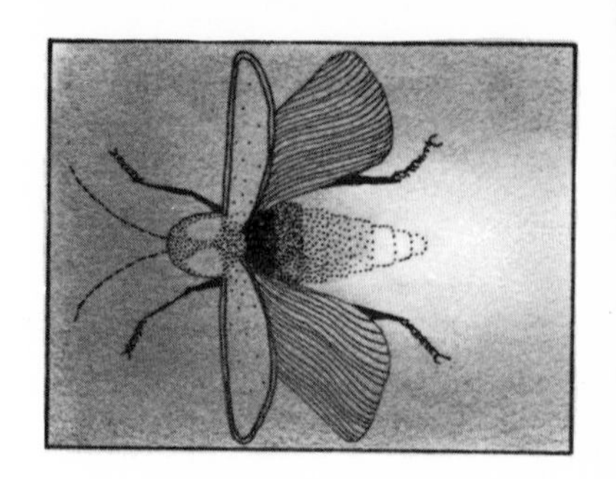

NIGHT TRAVEL

Two things fly in the dark of the night
And carry with them a lovely light.
One is the firefly,
Low in the grasses,
The other the aeroplane
Up where it passes.
Bats fly, too, and owls can roam,
But they have no light to light them home.

Marchette Chute

NOCTURNE

The three-toed tree toad
Sings his sweet ode
  To the moon:
The funny bunny
And his honey
  Trip in tune.
The gentle cricket
From his thicket
  Lifts his croon;
A love-lorn owlet
Of his fowlet
  Begs a boon.
Across the water
To her daughter
  Calls the loon;

A happy froglet
From his boglet
  Chants his rune.
The yellow hound-dog
And the brown dog
  Bay the 'coon;
The chipmunk dozes
Where the rose's
  Leaves are strewn;

All through the night-time
Till the bright time
  Comes, too soon,
The three-toed tree toad
Sings his sweet ode
  To the moon.

Arthur Guiterman

QUESTIONS AT NIGHT

Why
Is the sky?

What starts the thunder overhead?
Who makes the crashing noise?
Are the angels falling out of bed?
Are they breaking all their toys?

Why does the sun go down so soon?
Why do the night-clouds crawl
Hungrily up to the new-laid moon
And swallow it, shell and all?

If there's a Bear among the stars,
As all the people say,
Won't he jump over those Pasture-bars
And drink up the Milky Way?

Does every star that happens to fall
Turn into a fire-fly?
Can't it ever get back to Heaven at all?

And why
Is the sky?

Louis Untermeyer

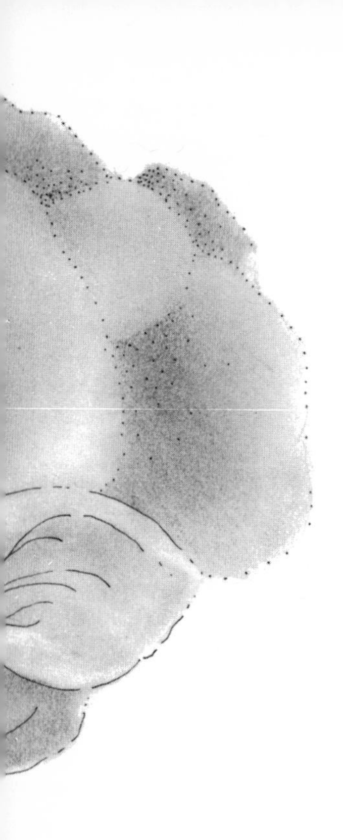

WINDY NIGHTS

Whenever the moon and stars are set,
   Whenever the wind is high,
All night long in the dark and wet,
   A man goes riding by.
Late in the night when the fires are out,
Why does he gallop and gallop about?

Whenever the trees are crying aloud,
   And ships are tossed at sea,
By, on the highway, low and loud,
   By at the gallop goes he.
By at the gallop he goes, and then
By he comes back at the gallop again.

Robert Louis Stevenson

NIGHT LANDSCAPE

Rolling and tossing out sparkles like roses
puffing out plum-coloured smoke as it goes is
a cedarwood train
on an ebony plain
whose passenger muses or gazes or dozes

the boy on the train is guard, passenger, driver
who reads while he drives, while the train, like a diver,
soars, plunges, and swoops
describes hundreds of loops
all veiled in its vapour like Lady Godiva

the boy is the track is the train is the cedar
from which it was carved, is the book, is the reader
who turns out the light
and shoots into night
and spends all his dream playing follow-my-leader

Joan Aiken

Peddling
From door to door
Night sells
Black bags of peppermint stars
Heaping cones of vanilla moon
Until
His wares are gone
Then shuffles homeward
Jingling the gray coins
Of daybreak.

from *Four Glimpses of Night*
by *Frank Marshall Davis*